FULL COUNT

by Lisa Moore

illustrated by Roberta Collier-Morales

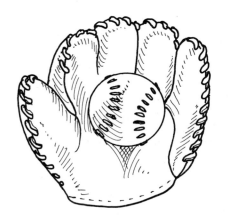

Harcourt

Orlando   Boston   Dallas   Chicago   San Diego

Visit *The Learning Site!*

www.harcourtschool.com

When people first hear about Frankie Mercer, they automatically assume she is a boy—until they meet her; her real first name is Francesca. When people inquire about her nickname, she informs them she's named for her paternal grandfather, Francis Bartholomew Ryan III, whom everyone knew as Frankie. From 1939 to 1945, he played for the Chicago American Giants, one of the greatest teams in the Negro National League. A

photograph of the 1940 team graces the Mercers' mantle, with Frankie's grandpa in the front row, third from the left, displaying a wide grin. He was a powerhouse hitter, built more of conviction than brawn.

If you ask her father, he'll tell you that Frankie *really* was named after Frank Robinson, his boyhood hero. Robinson was the first African American manager of a major-league team; he skippered the Indians in 1974, the year Frankie's dad played varsity baseball in the suburbs of Cleveland.

Frankie's mother confesses that she's not sure who her daughter's namesake is, but after three sons, she had expected one more, so she and her husband hadn't bothered to choose a girl's name. Frankie is what she and her husband called her during the pregnancy, and that's who she became when she was born.

2

All three Mercer boys play baseball, so Frankie had witnessed hundreds of games. Jason, the oldest, was a senior and played third base for the varsity team. Vincent was in ninth grade and was the team's catcher, and Doug was in seventh grade and pitched in the Babe Ruth League. Frankie never failed to cheer enthusiastically for her brothers. As for Frankie, she loved playing baseball, too. She wished she could go on to play baseball as her brothers did, but she had reached her last year on an official coed Little League team. After sixth grade, only softball was available to girls. In Frankie's estimation, this circumstance was grossly unfair.

She had decided, however, that if this was to be her last year of baseball, she would make the most of it. Frankie was a highly competent fielder, a devoted team player, and a good sport. At practice, she connected well and wisely avoided the high pitches. The trouble was, Frankie hadn't made a hit during a game all season. Most of the time she either swung at the air or stood like a statue and let the umpire call her out.

The boys on the team were always supportive and encouraging. "Come on, Frankie! You can do it!" they yelled every time she stepped up to the plate. Once, the score was 8 to 7, and Eddie Radcliffe was on third with two outs. Frankie had swung too late and lost the game. After that game, Coach Robert gave the Royals a post-game talk, never once blaming Frankie—but Frankie knew better.

Even though baseball flowed through Frankie Mercer's veins, she occasionally felt self-conscious about being the only girl on the team. She also knew she lacked confidence in her skill at bat. Despite this, another reason Frankie had been determined to remain in Little League this year was because her best friend since third grade, Lacey Everett, had promised to be on the team, too. "Sure, it'll be awesome," Lacey chirped as she smeared a glob of lip gloss across her mouth with an index finger. Frankie frowned at Lacey; she considered makeup a big waste of allowance.

Ultimately, Lacey had elected to abandon baseball for cheerleading. She didn't break the news to Frankie gently, or even sheepishly. One Friday night, when Lacey was sleeping over at Frankie's, she blurted out, "I quit the team today."

Frankie almost *never* cried, but now her eyes filled with tears. Frankie was crying for two reasons: because she didn't want to be the only girl on the team and because she didn't want to quit. Frankie loved grass stains, fly balls, and unpredictable grounders. She even loved sitting on

the bench. Most of all, she liked her teammates and her coach.

Frankie had been feeling demoralized by her performance all season, and Lacey's announcement made her feel even worse.

"Come on, cheer up!" urged Lacey. "You know, I don't mean to put you down, but you haven't been having the best luck on the baseball field. Why don't you join the cheerleading squad? You'd look great out there, and besides, you're so coordinated and..."

Frankie interrupted Lacey with a loud honk as she blew her nose. "Lacey, I can't believe you," sobbed Frankie. "I'm really hurt. First, you quit the team out of the blue, after you committed to playing all season, and then you insult my ball playing and urge *me* to be a quitter, too? What kind of friend are you?"

"Hey, don't get so touchy, OK? I was just offering you an alternative to feeling weird about being the only girl on the team."

"Well, I'm not quitting; that's certainly no solution, and the least you can do is show some support."

"OK, OK, you're right. I'm sorry I didn't think about your feelings before I left the team. I just wanted to try cheerleading, and some of the practices and competitions interfere with the baseball schedule. Of course, I'll still go to every single game I can and cheer you on, Frankie." Lacey gave her a hug.

"Thanks," sniffed Frankie.

On one particular Sunday afternoon in May—two days after Lacey quit—Frankie Mercer sat on the bench, now the only girl on the team. She fully expected to keep making outs; after all, as her social studies teacher, Ms. Duncan, always said, "History is bound to repeat itself."

Royals: After 5 games	AB	BB	H	BA
Arias, Ramon	19	3	5	.263
Creedon, Mike	15	1	3	.200
~~Everett, Lacey~~				
Forsythe, Zeke	17	2	3	.176
Margolin, Sam	21	1	10	.476
Mercer, Frankie	2	9	0	.000

Their first game in the play-offs was against the Blue Jays. Before the game Coach Robert had posted a current batting statistics sheet in the dugout. As Frankie stared with wide eyes at those three enormous zeros beside her name, a feeling of shame washed over her.

By the bottom of the final inning, the score was 14 to 13. Every Royal—except Frankie, of course—had gotten a hit: six singles, three doubles, a triple, and two home runs. The score seesawed, but now the Royals were behind. There was only one out, and Gary Zuchegno was on first base.

Coach Robert leaned over as Frankie stepped from the on-deck circle. "The pitcher's getting tired," he said, motioning toward the mound. "Keep your eye on the ball and be patient. Remember, a walk is as good as a hit."

Frankie tapped the heavy rubber doughnut off her bat and tossed it toward the bench. Zeke Forsythe grabbed it on the roll and said, "You can do it, Frankie!"

Frankie glanced around the infield. It was her third time up; she'd already struck out twice. As soon as they saw her, the infield players shifted left, looking for the double play. "Easy out!" an outfielder yelled. Frankie shot him an intimidating look, but he just yelled more obnoxiously.

The pitcher, Jeremy Leisher, was a lanky blond boy who towered close to six feet tall. He had a unique delivery—wobbly in the stretch—but he could throw the ball 60 miles per hour. The coach was right; Jeremy *was* looking a little ragged. Gary Zuchegno had swung at an outside pitch on a 3–0 count. Luckily, he punched it past the third baseman. The right fielder efficiently nabbed it, but Gary's foot stomped the base before the ball smacked into the first baseman's glove.

Frankie tapped her bat and turned to the catcher, a stocky boy with shocks of red hair sticking out of the sides of his protective mask. When he met her gaze, he chewed his gum harder and spit through the mask. "She's no batter!" he yelled at the infield.

Frankie took a few practice swings; on the third swing, she pointed the bat at the pitcher and attempted to scowl.

The pitcher bent down, staring intently at the catcher, who offered a sign. The umpire gave the signal, and Frankie gulped air and held it in her lungs until the ball left the pitcher's grip. It was so far outside that the catcher nearly toppled over. Frankie heard the umpire call, "Ball one!" She relaxed, stepped out of the box, and looked to Coach Robert. "Good eye!" he hollered.

Frankie had walked nine times that season, more than any of her teammates. Half the reason was her patience; the other half was that when she hesitated, assuming that she'd strike out, she was just playing the odds that the pitcher couldn't throw three strikes.

As she lifted her bat again, the pitcher nodded no and then yes to his catcher. Jeremy licked his lips, spit into the dirt, and pitched from the stretch. When it came in straight and fast, Frankie pondered too much. When she swung, it was half-hearted and half a second too late.

"Steeeeerike!" the umpire yelled. He held up one finger on each hand, and Frankie tasted the familiar sourness of embarrassment and disappointment.

"Come on, Frankie!" Coach Robert yelled. "Don't think, just swing!"

Frankie felt feverish and unfocused; she looked at Jeremy and thought, this guy doesn't have a lot of good pitches left in him. "Don't think, just swing," she repeated to herself over and over.

She actually was talking out loud when the next pitch arrived, and she swung with all her might. Level, hard, and strong, it was a good swing, a perfect swing...but there was no ball to hit; the ball was about a foot beyond the end of her bat, so far outside that it bounced against the backstop, and the catcher whipped off his face mask to chase it. As he did, Gary Zuchegno darted to second. The catcher threw with ferocity, but Gary had bustled, and he was safe. Frankie smiled—maybe Gary would steal his way home and tie things up.

"One and two!" the umpire signaled. Frankie stepped out of the box again, and Coach Robert approached. "See the hole?" he asked, pointing between the shortstop and the third baseman.

"Yeah," she answered uncertainly, sniffing.

"You can do it, Frankie," he encouraged. "Pretend it's batting practice," he suggested.

"Yeah, sure," she said, wiping her arm across her forehead.

"Let's go!" yelled the umpire, consulting his watch. The sunset was a rosy swirl of clouds in a blue and red sky, like a painting. As Frankie looked up, she thought it mirrored her emotions: swirls of excitement, fear, hope, and humiliation—all bright as neon.

"Go, Frankie!" squealed Lacey's voice from the stands.

Frankie stepped up to the plate again. Gary Zuchegno was poised on second. She stared at the pitcher, who glared back. "Hey, Frankie!" he jeered. "Take this!" He wound up, threw vigorously, and she swung, half hoping she would miss so that this ordeal would finally end.

Frankie felt the connection as a jolt in her shoulders and watched the ball soar in a wondrous arc. The faces of the crowd rose in the dusk, as if they were watching a tiny white bird flying toward the maple trees beyond the outfield. Frankie held her breath; the spectators in the stands cheered and stamped their feet against the metal bleachers, waving their arms. Almost in unison, her teammates shouted, "Run!"

Frankie dropped her bat and ran as fast as she could, trying not to watch the ball. Her heart pounded as hard as her cleats, her braids slapped her shoulders, and her hat flew off as she pushed her muscles to go, go, go...

"Foul ball!" the umpire yelled. The crowd emitted a collective groan.

Frankie overran the base, breathless and frustrated. As the ball rolled toward the sidewalk, the left fielder trotted to retrieve it. The first baseman, a stubby kid with braces said, "Nice hit." Frankie just looked at her feet.

As she returned to home, she spotted Lacey near the bench, talking to Bryan Pringle, the Royals' first baseman. Lacey laughingly punched Bryan on the shoulder. Bryan laughed, too. Frankie assumed they were laughing at her. She clenched her teeth and kicked the dirt; she almost wished the left fielder had snagged that ball.

On the way back, she reached over to fetch her hat. She slapped it against her leg and yanked it on with a jerk. The people in the stands were sitting again, and the fielders were restless. The sky got redder and redder. Somewhere in the distance a siren screeched.

Coach Robert met her at the plate. "Way to connect," he said, but Frankie was weary of his optimism. She was tired of being told constantly that she could do it when, in fact, she couldn't. Her batting average conveyed it: she was a big zero. Despite all her desires and know-how, she just couldn't hit. Her coach kept talking, but it sounded as if he were in an adjoining room.

The count was still one and two when she stepped back to the plate. The pitcher wiped his forehead on his arm as he leaned over to see the catcher's sign. Frankie resumed her stance, lifting her elbow high and bending her knees. The next pitch was way outside, and, thankfully, she had enough control and restraint not to swing. The umpire yelled, "Ball two."

Frankie's father yelled, "You can do it, Frankie!" Mr. Mercer faithfully came to every game. He left his job at the newspaper early and paced the first-base line the whole time, too nervous to sit still. He scrutinized every pitch and play as if it were the World Series, and after every game he took her to the Goshen Dairy for a cone. He always ordered strawberry; she, chocolate. He shouted, "Double scoops for a hit, Frankie!" and her face reddened.

The next pitch hummed at her knees. She waited uncertainly for the umpire to call it a strike (it was close) so that this humiliation would cease. Instead, he yelled, "Low! Ball three!" She heard the umpire's plastic pitch-counter click and stepped out of the batter's box to retie her cleat. She hoped it would distract the pitcher enough to throw another ball. A walk would be salvation; Jimmy Robert was up next, and he had the best average on the team.

The Blue Jays' coach called a time-out and sauntered to the infield. The pitcher left the mound, and they conferred. The pitcher shook his head yes and then no. The coach squatted on the ground and drew something in the grass. The pitcher snapped gum, blew a pink bubble, and nodded yes.

In the meantime, Frankie Mercer thought about Lacey Everett. Then she thought about quitting the team. The guys might even be glad if she quit, she thought. Even though she was an awesome shortstop, Mike Creedon was taller, and he'd be ecstatic to take over her position. Maybe Lacey was right; she should trade her cleats for saddle shoes and her glove for pom-poms and...

"Play ball!" the umpire ordered. Unfortunately, she couldn't quit just yet.

Frankie sighed hard, tapped the bat on the plate, swung it three times, and then waited, watching the pitcher frown. He released, and she could tell it was good. She closed her eyes, swung…and connected with a whack, dropped the bat, and took off toward first, propelled by her own disbelief. Then she turned toward second. She was vaguely aware that Gary Zuchegno was crossing home plate as the crowd erupted. The umpire yelled, "Foul ball!" just as she hit second; the ball had plopped beyond third base, about a foot foul. Again, the crowd groaned. As she trotted past Jeremy, he sneered, "Tough luck."

Now Frankie was furious. This involved too much emotion and way too much effort. She was definitely quitting now. Why should she continue this agony? Wasn't baseball supposed to be fun? This was about as much fun as getting a cavity filled—and it was lasting that long, too. She could hit ten more foul balls and still manage to lose the game.

It was a long way back this time. Frankie walked with her head down. The full count—*three balls and two strikes*—weighed heavily upon her. She knew whatever happened next was up to her.

Then she heard a sound. It started off soft and slow and then increased to loud and fast. At first, she thought the crowd was shouting, "Yankee! Yankee!" her all-time favorite team, and then she realized it was her name. Coach Robert and her teammates were stomping and chanting her name, too. Gary Zuchegno, now back on second, chimed in. All the fans were on their feet, the metal bleachers rumbling with their hopefulness, hands clapping, voices cheering, "Fran-KEE! Fran-KEE!" It was as if she were in Yankee Stadium and it were the World Series—and everyone was counting on her. Frankie felt as if she were riding a wave. The young ballplayer realized how much everyone believed in her, and she decided right then and there that, most important of all, *she* believed in Frankie Mercer, too! She ran the last few steps to home plate and grabbed her bat.

Frankie felt her blood rise to the sound, her heart in perfect sync with the chant. She squeezed the bat, gritted her teeth, and screamed to the pitcher, "Come on, buddy! Give me something to hit!" He released a pitch that was straight and chest high and—thanks to all those other pitches—as slow and manageable as honey.

Frankie swung, for what seemed like the hundredth time that day, but this time she experienced the difference as soon as she connected. She felt what baseball players have been feeling for 125 years: the exhilaration of simply clobbering a baseball with a bat and reveling in the run toward first base. As she surged ahead, the chanting was replaced by an uproarious explosion of joy. As she rounded first, she saw the ball drop into the outfield, far beyond the hole for which she'd been aiming. As her third-base coach signaled to hold her at second, she stopped short, panting and grinning. She'd done it!

The score was tied; Frankie Mercer was safe. No more triple zeroes. Now Jimmy Robert stepped up to bat.